A pretty good team

by Penny Anderson
illustrated by Richard Wahl

THE CHILD'S WORLD

ELGIN, ILLINOIS 60120

Library of Congress Cataloging in Publication Data

Anderson, Penny S.
  A pretty good team.

  (Handling difficult times)
  SUMMARY: When Jeff's parents decide to divorce,
Jeff and his mother plan to live together in an
apartment.
  [1. Divorce—Fiction]   I. Wahl, Richard.
II. Title.   III. Series.
PZ7.A54875Pr   [Fic]   79-15928
ISBN 0-89565-097-5

Distributed by Childrens Press, 1224 West Van Buren Street,
Chicago, Illinois 60607.

A pretty good team

Mom and Dad were fighting again. Oh, how Jeff wished they'd stop! They didn't fight much in the daytime. Dad wasn't around. But when he was home, he said things like, "It would be nice to have clean socks sometimes." He acted as though he were talking to Jeff, but really he was talking to Mom. Mom just pretended not to hear.

When Mom wasn't watching TV, she moved around the house with a half smile on her face. It was as though she knew a secret no one else knew. It wasn't a happy smile. It made Jeff feel lost and alone. That's the way he felt most of the time, lost and alone.

When Mom came in from work, she tried to act as if everything were fine. But she didn't talk to Jeff the way she had before. She didn't listen either. When Dad got home, she didn't talk at all. She hummed a strange little song to herself. She smiled that sad, secret smile.

That night, Mom and Dad talked to each other after Jeff went to bed. At first, they talked in low tones. Jeff couldn't hear what they were saying, no matter how hard he tried. But the talking grew louder and louder. Jeff didn't want to hear then. He put his pillow over his head. He still could hear them yelling.

Jeff remembered how it was before the fighting began. He'd wake up early and run into Mom and Dad's room, telling them it was time to get up. They were always happy and laughing. Jeff would watch Dad shave. Then he would help Mom put the dishes in the dishwasher after breakfast.

After that, he would go to school, while Mom and Dad went to work. That's the way it had been before.

Why had everything changed?

Jeff worried a lot about that. He thought about it most of the time. He thought about it when he should have been working in his workbook. He thought about it at night. He thought about it when he was supposed to finish his arithmetic problems. Jeff even thought about it at lunchtime. Then he wasn't hungry anymore.

Jeff heard his name sometimes when his parents were fighting. Maybe it was his fault. He couldn't think of anything he had done to make them so mad, but. . .

Nothing was right anymore. Finally, Jeff fell asleep with his head under his pillow. A sound woke him, much later. It was a door banging shut, so hard it shook the house.

The next day at school was a bad day for Jeff. His stomach hurt all morning. Then, before he knew it, he was throwing up, all over his desk.

Jeff hated to go home after school. He hated to tell Mom what had happened.

"Mom. . ." he began.

"Mmmm," she answered.

"Mom. . . I threw up today. It was awful. . ."

Jeff stopped. Mom was just sitting there, staring at the TV, at a dumb quiz show.

"You don't even care!" Jeff shouted. He ran into his room and banged the door. Hard.

Mom came running. "Jeffrey, what is the matter? Why did you bang your door like that? Answer me!"

Jeff rolled under his bed and flattened himself against the wall. He did not answer. If Mom had listened, she would know what was the matter.

"You are impossible! Just like your father!" she yelled.

Jeff stuck his fingers in his ears and closed his eyes.

"Maybe you should live with him when we get the divorce!" she yelled. With that, she stomped out, slamming the door again.

13

Divorce? What was that all about? A divorce?

Jeff took his fingers out of his ears. He curled up in a tight ball against the wall.

Divorce? Joe's parents had gotten a divorce. Joe was Jeff's best friend last year. But now, Joe wanted to fight all the time. Maybe the divorce was what made Joe fight.

Jeff felt like fighting, too, but what good would it do? It didn't help Joe at all. None of his friends liked him any more.

Mindy's parents were divorced, but Mindy didn't seem to mind. At least she didn't fight all the time. She did cry easily, but Jeff had always thought that was because she was a girl. Now, though, he felt like crying too.

A long time later, Jeff felt someone pulling on his shirt. "Jeff, Jeff, wake up. Wake up and come out from under your bed. Please, Jeff. I want to talk to you."

It was Mom. She was halfway under the bed, pulling on his shirt. She was crying.

"Please, Jeff honey, come out and talk to me. We need to talk."

Jeff crawled out. He blinked at the light that had been turned on in his room. He must have cried himself to sleep. It was night. He could smell dinner cooking in the kitchen.

Mom sat down on the edge of his bed. Tears slipped down her cheeks. She held her arms out to him. Jeff flung himself against her and buried his face in her shoulder. They cried together. Mom rocked them back and forth.

"Oh, Jeff, I'm sorry. I am so mixed up and unhappy! I didn't realize you felt the same way. I've been too busy with my own problems. I haven't even thought about yours. Oh, Jeff, I AM sorry. . ."

"That's O.K., Mom," Jeff said, hugging her tightly. It felt good to be near her again.

"No, it's not O.K.," Mom answered. "We need to talk. When you slammed the door, I was mad at you. I thought you were shutting me out of your life. Then I realized, that's just what Dad and I have done to you. We've shut you out, while we've fought about our troubles."

"Why do you fight? You never used to. . . much."

"I hate your father!"

Jeff stiffened at the anger in his mother's voice.

"I hate him because he wants a divorce. I guess I'll have to give it to him. We can't go on fighting like this. I can't stand it."

"Are you mad at me too?" Jeff asked. "What did I do?" His throat ached.

"Oh, no. You didn't do anything, son. It isn't your fault. We aren't mad at you at all."

"Then why does Dad want a divorce? Whose fault is it? Doesn't he love us anymore?"

"He loves you, Jeff. He just doesn't love me. And it's probably both his fault and mine. Dad and I just can't get along anymore."

Mom was silent for a moment, then she said, "Your father doesn't want to live here with us. He'll pick up his things tomorrow. I'm not sure we can live here either. It will be too expensive, even with Dad sending us money."

"Where will you go? Will I go with you?"

"Oh, yes, Jeff. You will live with me. Dad and I have agreed on that. I'm not sure where we'll live. But you can help me find an apartment both of us like. Will you do that?"

Jeff nodded. Mindy lived in an apartment, and she liked it. "Where will Dad live?" he asked.

"Dad's company will send him to Indiana soon. He'll live there."

JEFF

"All alone?"

Mom pressed her lips tightly together. "No. He won't be alone. He's going to live with Uncle Joe for awhile. Then he'll get his own place."

"But I want him here to live with us."

"I know. But Dad and I are getting a divorce. Divorce means he won't be married to me anymore, so we won't live together. He'll still be your father, though, for always."

"Will I see him again?"

"You can see him tomorrow when he comes for his things. And I'm sure he'll want to see you whenever he can. You can visit him on your vacations."

Joe did that. . .visited his father on vacations.

"I'm sorry things worked out this way, Jeff," said his mother. She began to cry again.

"Don't cry, Mom. It will be all right. We'll be O.K. I can help you, Mom, and you can help me. We'll get along. You'll see. We'll make a good team."

Mom looked at him the way she used to. She smiled. . .a real smile this time. "You know, Jeff, I think you're right. We're a pretty good team. We'll get along."

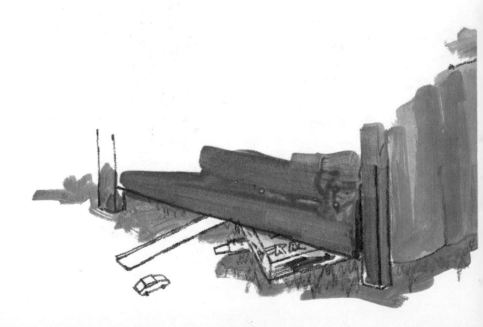

JEFF

THINKING AND TALKING

Jeff has been through a hard time, hasn't he? Often, when parents get a divorce, the hardest time of all is before they decide to do it. That's when all the fighting goes on.

There will be more hard times for Jeff. He will miss his Dad in between visits. Jeff will feel lonely sometimes and angry sometimes. He will wish his Dad would come back and live with him. But these hard times won't be as bad as not knowing what's wrong.

Jeff already knows a few things about getting a divorce. He knows both his parents are sad and angry. He knows now that the divorce is not his fault. A divorce is never the fault of children in the family.

Divorces happen for many, many reasons. Jeff knows that his mother and father couldn't get along. Sometimes that is the only reason for a divorce. Sometimes there are other reasons. Sometimes children know the reasons, and sometimes they don't.

Jeff feels sad about the divorce. That is all right. It will take time to get over feeling sad. And until he does, he needs some time alone. He needs help from friends. He needs to be with people who can make him laugh.

Jeff feels angry about the divorce too. All children feel angry after a divorce. Jeff may need some help in figuring out what to do about his anger.

There are several things to remember about anger. The first is that everyone gets angry sometimes. People don't need to be upset with themselves just because they get angry.

The second thing to remember is this. Bad thoughts don't hurt other people. They only hurt us. I might think, "I wish you were dead!"

But I don't need to be afraid that my angry thought will kill you.

Here is the third thing to remember. Angry thoughts don't hurt other people. But angry words can hurt them. And angry actions can hurt them. When we are angry, we need to be careful. We should say we are angry. And often we should tell people why we are angry. But we don't need to say nasty things, just because we are angry. And we don't need to break things.

Sometimes, we are so angry, we feel we must do something! Anything! Punching a pillow is a good thing to do when we're angry. So is punching a punching bag. What else can an angry person do? Remember, whatever he does should help him, but not hurt anyone else.

Sometimes, when we get angry, we do hurt

other people. We say mean things, then are sorry. Or we do mean things, then feel bad. When this happens, there is only one thing to do. It is hard. It takes courage. We must say, "I'm sorry." We must make things right.

Jeff may worry sometimes about being loyal. When parents get a divorce, children are stuck in the middle. Mom is angry at Dad. Dad is angry at Mom. But the best thing Jeff can do is love Mom and love Dad too. For they love him.

Most parents love their children. This love doesn't stop just because of a divorce. It keeps on going. Even the parent who is away will show love for the children. The parent may come to see them, or write, or call. There are many, many ways to show love.

Once in a while, though, parents do stop loving their children. This should never happen, but sometimes it does. It is a very sad happening. If it happens, children need to remember one thing. Every child deserves to be loved. If a parent can't love, it is because the parent is sick or weak or has a problem. It is not the child's fault, not ever. And even if a parent can't love a child, someone else will be able to love him.

After a time, life will settle back to normal for Jeff. Maybe he and his mother will live alone. Maybe she will marry again. Then Jeff will have to get used to a stepfather. Jeff's father may marry too. Then Jeff will have a stepmother as well. These things might seem strange at first. Jeff might feel angry again, or sad. But he'll get used to changes. And he'll get along just fine. After all, Jeff is loved a lot by both his Mom and his Dad.